RETURN TO BOOKMOBILE

GRANDMA'S GONE
TO LIVE IN THE STARS

MAX HAYNES

ALBERT WHITMAN & COMPANY
MORTON GROVE, ILLINOIS

Library of Congress Cataloging-in-Publication Data

Haynes, Max.
Grandma's gone to live in the stars / written and illustrated by
Max Haynes.
p. cm.
Summary: In the moments after
Grandmother has passed away,
her spirit is at peace
as she says goodbye
to her sleeping family and her home.

ISBN 0-8075-3026-3 (hardcover)
[1. Grandmothers—Fiction. 2. Death—Fiction.] I. Title.
PZ7.H3149149 Gr 2000
[E]—dc21   99-050902

Published in 2000 by
Albert Whitman & Company,
6340 Oakton Street, Morton Grove, Illinois 60053-2723.

Published simultaneously in Canada by General Publishing, Limited, Toronto.

Printed in the United States of America.

10 9 8 7 6 5 4 3 2 1

For Catherine, and your grandma, too.
Shine on.

I was so sick.
So sick that I died.
Now I feel . . . wonderful.
And now it's time to say
goodbye.

Goodbye, Son.

Goodbye, Daughter.

Goodbye, Child.

Goodbye, Baby.

So long, Cat.

Goodbye, Dog.

Goodbye, Pictures.

Goodbye, Children,

one more time.

Goodbye, Garden.

Goodbye, Town.

Goodbye, Earth.

Hello, Stars.